# The Adventures of Mahalia and Malcolm

by
Terance Shipman     Prudence Williams

Copyright @ 2021
Team Shipman Publishing Ellenwood, Georgia
All Rights Reserved

No part of this work may be reproduced or transmitted in any form or by any means, electronic or mechanical, including photocopying and recording, or by any information storage or retrieval system without the prior written permission of Team Shipman Publishing unless such copying is expressly permitted by federal copyright law. Address inquiries to Team Shipman Publishing, 2700 Silver Queen Rd Ellenwood, Georgia 30294

# Forward

Growing up during the '70s, I remember putting on a blue towel and pretending to be Batman. Batman is still my favorite superhero. I didn't see many Black superheroes while growing up. Maybe once a year, I would catch Black Lightning on "Super Friends". I would see Falcon and Power Man (Luke Cage) in comics. The two black heroes that changed everything were Storm of the "X-Men" and Cyborg of "New Teen Titans". They took Black heroes to a whole new level. It was a good feeling to read and see not only two new Black superheroes but also two powerful characters.

Okay, I know everyone's wondering, "What about Black Panther?" Well, when I was growing up, I knew about him from the superhero encyclopedia, but not in the comics. He wasn't there when I was growing up.

Today the world is flooded with Black superheroes: in comics, on television, in books, and movies. So, why *The Adventures of Mahalia and Malcolm?* I want to tell my story of a Black family of superheroes. My family has always been very important to me. I am who and what I am because of what others have done before me. I wanted to make a family with a history of superpowers. The books will show the love, pain, and growth of one family, the Robinsons. I hope you enjoy *The Adventures of Mahalia and Malcolm.*

Sincerely,
**TERANCE L. SHIPMAN**

# Dedication

This superhero book is dedicated to my super team, my children. My five children are Jerontai, Teryn, Zaire, BJ, and Khalil. As a father, I have dedicated my life to them. I try to be the best father I can be. I have fallen short many days, but I get back up because I know they are watching. As a parent, I have prayed for love, strength, patience, and wisdom when raising children. I always talk to my children about putting God first, staying united as a family, earning something no one can take away from you: an education, and the power of hard work, for which there is no substitute. This book is to all of you, my superheroes.

Love your father,
**TERANCE L. SHIPMAN**

# Section 1

# The Dinner

"Junior, why do you drive that car so fast? Your hot rod will never be as fast as me!" Olivia Robinson declared, using her super speed to outrun her son's car up the driveway. She was excited to have him home. He'd been traveling the world for several months. Tonight, the family, well at least most of the family, would be celebrating his return. She'd been cooking all day in preparation and had fixed all his favorites.

"Hi, beautiful lady," Junior said. "I missed you so much." They hugged and smiled at each other.

Olivia Robinson looked at her handsome son and said, "I missed you too, baby."

"Mom, I brought some soft drinks for the dinner," Junior said, reaching into the trunk of his car and holding up several twenty-four packs of sodas.

"Yeah, your dad will love that," Olivia said taking the boxes from him. Then she looked at him and reprimanded, "But slow that car down and turn that music down too! I felt that bass five minutes before I saw your car."

"Oh mom, you know you like that bass." Junior laughed. That had always been one of his joys, vibrant, booming rap music. His mom might quip about it, but he knew she enjoyed his music too. She just didn't like it as loud as he did.

"Yeah, I've still got a move or two," Olivia said, showing off her dance moves and dancing with her son.

They both turned at movement coming from the doorway. A fluff of brown hair surrounded a teen angel's face. "Uncle Junior!" said Mahalia, as she ran up to kiss him.

"How's my favorite niece?" Junior asked, looking at his pretty niece. She was 13 and becoming a beautiful woman, with big eyes, a cute button nose, and a beautiful smile.

Laughing and looking at him with a big smile, Mahalia quipped, "I'm, your only niece."

Her uncle gave her his million-dollar smile, and draped his arm across her shoulder, "You're still my favorite. Now, where are Dad and Malcolm?"

"They're outside in the garden," Mahalia said.

Junior nodded and asked, "So where are your parents?"

"They went to the store for Grandma," Mahalia said while using her cell phone to snap a quick selfie of her uncle and herself.

Olivia watched as her granddaughter waved her hand over the screen of her cell phone and magically decorated the picture she'd just taken with animal ears and a frothy pink and blue sparkling background.

"That's good!" Olivia said, praising her granddaughter's use of her powers to manipulate digital systems. She was so engaged with her granddaughter that she barely noticed Junior stride towards the back of the house in search of his dad and nephew.

When Junior entered the backyard, he noticed his mother's vegetable and flower garden. Sunflowers grew at least 10 feet high, and roses lined the garden's perimeter. Tomatoes and peppers grew in pots, and fat cucumbers and squash hung off vines. Next to them, rows of collard greens and kale flourished in bright green hues. Birds sang happily as Junior caught sight of his father standing and greeted him, "Hi, great father of mine."

Marshall looked up and smiled at his son. Turning his hands so that his palms faced the sky, Marshall waved his fingers in a gesture that summoned his son to him. His fingers radiated a wonderful golden light causing the ground under Junior to respond, form a mound of earth that rose and carried Junior across the 20 yards that separated them.

"Mom is going to kill you about her yard," Junior said as the mound settled and delivered him face to face with his father.

Reaching out, Marshall hardily hugged his son and said, "Hi son, it is good to see my baby boy."

"Good to see you too, dad; you're looking good."

"I have to stay in shape to keep up with these grandchildren," Marshall said. And indeed, he was in good shape for his age. In his late fifties, he could still run five miles a day with no problem and enjoyed working out at least twice a day.

"Malcolm! Come give me a hug, boy!" Junior said looking at the sprout of a boy that stood on the other side of the garden, waving his hand over a rose that slowly changed colors from red to blue and then to green. Malcolm looked in the direction of his uncle. Junior waved his hand over the rose in the opposite direction, and the bloom gracefully faded into a red hue once again. He briefly inspected the flower then raced across the garden and stopped in front of his uncle and grandfather.

"Hi, Uncle Junior!" Malcolm said. Malcolm playfully jabbed at his uncle. Uncle Junior laughed, easily dodge his punches, quickly spun his nephew around, and wrapped him in a headlock.

"Now boy, you know you can't sucker punch me," Junior said, tickling his nephew and asking, "How's my favorite nephew?" "And I know, you're my only one, but you're still my favorite." Junior released the slim boy who had a sharp chin and handsome smile.

"I'm good. Grandpa and I are practicing."

"Dad, you're teaching the kid how to do what?" Junior asked.

"He must learn to use his powers early. He must be trained to have self-control." Marshall stated, looking from son to grandson.

"You're right, he's got to learn. He's going to do great things one day and has to know how to control his powers to keep others and himself safe." Junior said. Then he looked at Malcolm and said, "You are very blessed. I wish I had powers."

Marshall eyed his son and reassured him, "Well son, your greatest power is your mind."

"I know," Junior sighed, "I just wish I could do something." Marshall was getting ready to respond and encourage his son to just be great at being himself when he heard the garden's gate open and saw Aaron and Cassandra enter.

Aaron, a heavy-set guy with kind eyes and an easy smile, surveyed the garden and noticed the overturned soil. He chuckled to himself as he realized that his dad had been showing off again. Shaking his head, he shouted towards his family, "Brother, when did you get here?" Excited to see his younger brother, Aaron jogged over and hugged Junior.

"I haven't been here long," Junior said. He stepped back and eyed his brother's burly frame, noticing that his brother was bigger and rounder in the midsection than he'd been the last time he'd seen him.

"Look at you!" Aaron said. "You've been working out! Are you still training in Jeet Kun Doo?"

"Yeah! Always keeping my body in shape. And it looks like Cassandra has been feeding you well."

"Yeah, the wife cooks all the time, and I eat everything she cooks!" Aaron said. They both laugh out loud.

Cassandra, a pretty, walnut-colored woman with wavy shoulder-length brown hair finally joined the conversation and laughed, "Well, look you at Junior."

Junior smiled and hugged her. "How are you, Cassandra?"

"I'm doing fine. Taking care of your brother and those two kids."

Junior reached out and squeezed one side of his brother's pudgy waist, "Yeah, I see my brother has gained weight."

Pushing Junior's hand off her husband's waist, Cassandra gave Junior a stern look, hugged her husband lovingly, and giggled, "He loves my cooking. And I love him."

"Yes, I do, sweetheart," Aaron said, looking at his brother. "Junior, you just mad you don't have nobody to cook for you every day!" They all laughed as Aaron pulled his wife closer, and Junior raised his hand in surrender.

"Now that everyone is here," Malcolm said, "I'm ready to eat!"

"Me too!" said Marshall. "Let's go see if your grandma has the food ready." Everyone turned to the French doors that led into the house and walked into the smell of good food.

"Is dinner ready?" Malcolm shouted when he saw his grandmother turn the corner and stepping into the kitchen.

Cassandra shushed him. "Stop yelling, Malcolm, your grandmother's right here." Then she turned and looked at her mother-in-law with a smile, "Hi Olivia, do you need help with anything because apparently, our guys are starving!"

Olivia laughed and lovingly rubbed the top of her grandson's head, before she said, "Thank you Cassandra, but dinner is ready and almost fully laid out on the table. Mahalia is finishing up right now! All I need ya'll to do is get washed up and go sit down."

All the men made a move toward the kitchen sink, but Olivia raised her hands, motioning them to stop. "We have enough bathrooms in this house for everyone to use a bathroom ... not my kitchen sink."

The men and Malcolm all look sheepish as they ambled out the kitchen in search of bathrooms.

Moments later, the whole family sat at the table holding hands. "Mahalia, bless the food please," her grandmother said.

Bowing her head, Mahalia spoke, "God, thank You for the food we are about to receive, and our daily bread. And God thank you for bringing Uncle Junior home safely." Quietly, the family chorused, "Amen."

Then they all started eating. Malcolm was the first to reach for the barbeque ribs his grandfather had been smoking all morning long. Forking up a half slab from the platter, he shot a quick look at his mom to see if she was going to say he was getting too much, but she didn't seem to notice. Next, he went for the collard greens his grandma had taken from the garden and cooked today. They had the house smelling so good that he'd been thinking about them all day. And that potato salad his mom had brought was his favorite, with bacon bits and onions.

Just as he was getting ready to scoop it up, a loud deafening sound erupted in the room, shaking the table. Boom!

The whole house vibrated. Plates scattered everywhere. Food was thrown into the air and landed all over the carpet. Just for a few seconds, Malcolm was stunned. Then he realized that he'd been thrown from his seat to the floor. Regaining his bearings, he looked around the room and saw his grandfather and uncle on the floor. They appeared to be unconscious. Mahalia laid next to him, moaning. He wasn't quite sure where his mom and dad were.

Feeling panic rise in his chest, Malcolm noticed that his grandmother had been knocked to the floor as well. She looked back over her shoulder to the source of the commotion. His gaze followed hers, and he saw it: the wall had been blown away. There were strangers in the house! WHAT IS HAPPENING!? His mind raced to try and comprehend everything that was happening.

"Oh my God," Malcolm thought, finally noticing that some type of bullet darts was hanging out his grandparents' bodies. "They'd been shot and drugged." However, the poison wasn't affecting Grandma Olivia like it affected Grandpa! She had quickly recovered and was already moving to protect the family. "Must be her super speed and hypermetabolism," he thought as he watched his grandmother swiftly shake off the effects of the drug and move as if she'd teleported across the room. Malcolm knew it wasn't teleportation; Grandma was just that fast!

"Who! What! NO!" Oliva thought as she lifted her eyes to the shattered wall. "Invaders! I must protect my family," she thought. Her heart was pounding and without hesitation, she moved. She moved as fast as she'd ever moved –faster than time allowed for most to move. In a flash, she had crossed the room, dismounted two swords that hung next to the family crest, and returned to stand against the invaders.

All Malcolm saw was his grandmother on the floor at one moment and standing with swords raised the next. Then he heard his grandfather's shout of terror.

"Oliva! Wait!" Marshall yelled. As soon as he said it, Malcolm saw his grandfather get shot with a dozen tranquilizer darts and fall to the ground.

Grandma Olivia slashed and stabbed, as she fought each approaching soldier. There were so many of them, but Grandma held her own. In fact, she was doing a lot of damage to them. Uncle Junior woke up, quickly jumped to his feet, and began fighting too. Even with very little power, he took down several invading warriors. His blows were powerful and well placed.

There's Dad, Malcolm realized, as he watched his father move to stand in front of his sister and mother.

"Malcolm, get over here!" Aaron yelled. At that call, Malcolm pushed himself across the floor and scrambled to be closer to this sister and mother, while his uncle and grandmother continued to fight.

"Whooaaa!" Malcolm thought. His eyes stretched wide just as his hand reached for his sister. Out of nowhere, a tall man wearing a scarlet-colored robe flew into the room. Neither Grandma nor Uncle Junior noticed the presence of the floating man; they were fighting so hard. However, Dad did and spread his body in an attempt to shield us from him. Grandpa just laid slump on the ground.

The man whose face was hidden behind the robe's hood levitated behind the fighting for several minutes. Then he bellowed, "Enough!"

His loud booming voice startled everyone. For a flash of a second, Grandma Oliva and Uncle Junior turned away from the fight and toward the voice. "No!" Malcolm yelled, but it was too late. He heard his mother and sister gasp. He jumped closer to them as he watched his grandma and uncle get hit with several darts.

"Grandma Olivia!" Mahalia cried. She tried to move towards Grandma but realized that Mom had her in a tight grip that she couldn't escape!

The hooded fly guy growled orders to the soldiers. "Don't worry about him," he said, looking down at Uncle Junior. "But hold her still! Don't let her get away!" he barked, as he loomed menacingly over Grandma Olivia. Just like before, the tranquilizer darts that they'd shot my grandmother with weren't enough to hold her down. She was already recovering, and she is already looking around, readying for the next round.

All eyes followed the Scarlet Robe, as he snarled out ominous words at my grandmother, "You don't know me." He stated in a hard voice, and then he added, with a menacing laugh, "I can tell it's driving you crazy. Your super memory won't help you now."

As Mahalia watched the floating red-robed jerk taunt our grandma, she could tell that grandma was mad! And not the usual Junior and his loud music or Grandpa raising the ground under her tulips type of mad. No, this was the kind of mad that made her eyes glow amber and her afro stand at full glory. It was the kind of mad that we had never seen, but Daddy had told us about in bedtime stories!

The Red-robed jerk continued to talk, picking at Grandma, "And Olivia, I see you've gotten slower with age. Years ago, I would have never captured you so easily." Grandma glared at him. I looked at Malcolm and could tell he saw the same thing I did. We both knew that Grandma was past mad; she was now plotting revenge. We saw it in her face. She assessed this crazy red housecoat-wearing weirdo for the sole reason of putting together a plan to kick his butt. Unfortunately, the guy didn't realize it as we did.

He looked over at us—Uncle Junior was still out cold on the floor, and Daddy was still using his body to shield us. I tried to see his face, but I couldn't. He said, "Your children and grandchildren—how beautiful they are. Mahalia and Malcolm, nice to meet you, finally."

Dad bowed up and lurched toward the foreigner. "Don't you speak to them! Don't look at them! And you better not ever touch them!" He said charging the man.

Evil Red Hood motioned to his goons, and without hesitation, they attacked Dad, hitting him in the head and knocking him to the floor. He fell into his mom's arms, unconscious.

The levitating idiot turned back to Grandma and said, "Let me show you the pain your husband caused me." He motioned for his soldiers to grab Dad again, and they slammed the end of their guns into my father's ribs. My mother cried. Even through her tears, she pressed her body against ours, refusing to let us up, denying us the opportunity to fight. She knew we could overcome her if we wanted, but she also knew, we wouldn't disobey her.

Red Robe turned to my grandmother again and said, "Bring her other weakling son to me." The goons grabbed Uncle Junior, dragged his unconscious body over, and dropped him in front of Grandma. One of them kicked Uncle Junior in the stomach, and he moaned.

Seeing both of her sons treated so badly galvanized Grandma, and she surged quickly, giving the soldiers holding her a hard time. They struggled to hold her down. "Sir, she's moving too fast," one of them grunted. Red Robe, mercilessly said, "Give her more darts!" They did. Several hit her in the legs and thighs, and a few more land in her chest. They didn't knock her out, but she was greatly subdued. She saw when the goons began kicking Uncle Junior in the chest and back and when they viciously stomp Dad's arms and legs.

Chuckling, Red Robe looked down at Dad and Junior, and said to Grandma, "They want powers like their father? Yet, they have no idea who your father is? I advise you to teach your sons to never try to fight me again! If they do, they will die." Quietly, he motioned his goons to leave Dad and Junior alone. He turned, looked at our slumping grandmother, and said, "I won't kill them ... today, Olivia."

Malcolm was terrified; he'd never seen Grandma cry, but the drugs from the darts weakened her. She couldn't get away. She wasn't able to fight. The only thing she could do at the moment

Robed Guy talked. Malcolm knew he should be listening. He knew it was important, so he focused on the man looking away from Grandma.

"Olivia?" Red Robe called as he hovered over her.

He paused for a few seconds and waited for her to respond.

"Do you feel my pain yet, Olivia?" he jeered. "Do you feel it?"

Grandma glared up at him, still crying, but she didn't utter a word. He paused and turned to Mom. She pushed her body hard against Mahalia and me, throwing her arms out wide, determined to protect us and hold us back at the same time.

"Cassandra, how are you?" Red Robe asked in a softer voice. Then he gently said, "She's my daughter, Olivia."

Mom didn't change her position. Still protecting us and holding us back at the same time, she cried, "No, you're not my father!"

Red Robe lowered himself to the floor. He stood boldly—then said in a plain and calm voice, "Yes, I am. How do you think I found you all?"

"No, No! You're not my father! I have no idea who you are, but you are not related to me, and you surely aren't my father!" Mom tried to argue, but Red Robe ignored it like he hadn't just throw some life-altering accusation out in the room.

He moved away from us, loomed in the air again, and floated towards Grandma. "Olivia," he said calmly, "I'm taking Marshall. He must pay for everything he has done to me." He paused and sighed. Finally, he said coldly, "First, I will take his powers. And then I will kill him with those powers."

He rose high in the air, almost touching the ceiling. He looked around the room and began to float towards the opening in the wall. His goons moved after him. Some had their guns pointed at us, keeping us in place, and four of the goons hauled Grandpa away.

Grandma was indeed drugged. The last dose they gave her seemed to really have slowed her down. She still couldn't fight. She still couldn't get away. All she could do was whisper, "Who are you?"

Red Robe floated away, as soldiers carried Grandpa in front of him, and more soldiers stood as guards behind him. Five soldiers still surrounded Grandma as he answered her question, "The one he never told you about but the one he hurt. I am the lost sheep!" He roared. Then he motioned to the soldiers holding Grandpa, "Take him to the plane." Without warning, he turned towards Mom. She pulled away, trying to increase the distance between her and this madman. He moved in close to her and whispered cynically, "Cassandra, my daughter, you will live today. I don't want my grandchildren to grow up without their mother." Mom turned her face, refusing to acknowledge him.

This didn't seem to bother Red Robe; he just nodded to the soldiers who shot Grandma in the leg again with the tranquilizer darts. "That should slow you down," he stated. Grandma still glared at him, her eyes raging. This seemed to annoy the intruder. He looked at the soldier and said, "Give her a few more darts." The goon closest to my grandmother shot her three more times … ping, ping, ping. Grandma's eyes slide close, and she crumpled into a heap. "That should put her to sleep," He announced.

Just like he'd done nothing wrong, Red Robe flew away with his soldiers behind him.

When they were gone, Cassandra and Malcolm raced to Grandma's side. Mahalia ran to the shattered wall and looked out at Red Robe and Grandpa. The soldiers entered a sleek aircraft and disappeared into the evening sky, leaving no evidence that they had even been there.

# Section 2

# The Recovery

Olivia was mad! As Malcolm and his mother, stared down at her, they could see it. The tranquilizer had begun to wear off. Her eyes were glowing almost golden now. She moved to push them away. Refusing both extended hands that would help her up, she stood on her own and surveyed the room. Junior and Aaron laid folded on the floor. The room was a mess, with the table broken and the wall gaping open. Mahalia stared through the hole into the night sky looking lost and confused.

Focusing her energy, Olivia wasted no time. Turning back to her grandson and his mother, she gave quick orders, "Cassandra, I'm ok! I need you to take care of Junior and Aaron! Malcolm, you stay with your mom and make sure she has what she needs!"

Then she shot across the room to Mahalia. "Mahalia, give me your phone," Olivia said, startling her granddaughter.

"Umm...What?" Mahalia stared, "Why do you need my cell phone?" Her face was incredulous.

"Mahalia!" Olivia thundered, eyes glowing, hand stretched out, "Phone! NOW!"

Mahalia had never seen her grandmother like this and immediately regretted her possessiveness towards her phone. She sighed, unlocked the screen, and handed the cell phone to her grandmother.

Mahalia watched as her grandmother tapped the screen and put the phone to her ear. The phone screen glowed, and Mahalia heard a voice answer, "Blue Pirate 12-28."

Her grandmother responded, "Panther13 ... Oak Tree Down!" Then she disconnected the call. She didn't wait for a response; she just hit the end button.

Handing Mahalia her phone, she pulled the girl into a tight embrace, "Baby, it's gonna be ok!" Grandma said, pressing her a hand into Mahalia's afro and kissing her on the forehead.

They walked back to the dining room, where they found Uncle Junior awake, but badly beaten, and Dad still unconscious. Malcolm stood behind Mom, looking little and scared, and Mom gently cleaned Dad's face with a napkin from the table.

Malcolm glanced up as his grandmother and Mahalia reentered the room. "What just happened?" Malcolm asked, his voice quivering. Grandma didn't answer. She just pulled me close, wrapped her arm around my shoulder, hugging me and Mahalia in one big warm embrace. I felt the tears in my eyes, and I tried my hardest not to cry, but I was scared. Whatever this was was bad!

"I want to do something Grandpa would do," Malcolm thought, "but I don't know what that is. Grandpa would have told me to protect the family, but he never really told me how, especially not in a situation where a crazy flying dude busts out the wall and shoots tranquilizer darts. And didn't that nut say he was mom's dad? Malcolm lowered his head. This is all too much," he thought. I just wanted potato salad and ribs.

Mom left the room and returned quickly with a wet towel in her hand and bandages hanging out of her pockets. She gave one towel to Grandma, and Grandma gently wiped the trail of blood from Dad's forehead. Dad's eyes opened to the soothing touch of the towel. He woke up, but he was in bad shape.

As Grandma helped Mom take care of Dad, Uncle Junior, and I walked over to Mahalia. She had kneeled on the floor next to them. Mom and Grandma focused on Dad and Uncle Junior, while I talked to Mahalia. "Mahalia," I whispered, "what happened? Who was that guy?" She's my big sister, and we don't always get along, but if she knew, she'd tell me the answer. She didn't know. She looked at me with eyes still full of tears.

"I have no idea!" She replied, "but Grandma said it's gonna be ok."

"You believe her?" I asked because I wanted so badly to believe everything is going to be ok but was having trouble believing it. I looked around again—Dad was moaning and swollen, and Uncle Junior was complaining about problems breathing.

"What's that sound?" Mahalia asked, jumping up and moving toward the hole in the wall. Before she could even take two steps, Grandma whizzed in front of her and told her to get back.

Mahalia grabbed Malcolm and pulled him close, and we watched as a helicopter landed in our yard. Malcolm strained to get away from me so he could see.

"Mahalia," he exclaimed. "That's an HH-60M Black Hawk!" I look at him grinning wide! "That's a military helicopter! They are built by Sikorsky, and their location is top secret, but they are owned by Lockheed Martin ... RIGHT HERE IN GEORGIA! And they use them for aerial reconnaissance and search and rescue too!"

I look at him, exasperated. "Malcolm! You're such a dork!" I hissed at my little brother, adding, "Who cares what kind of helicopter it is! I just hope they are here to take Dad and Uncle Junior to the hospital and to figure out who that creep who took Grandpa is!"

Malcolm looked correctly corrected. His eyes lowered, and he got quiet. "I guess this isn't the time to show my amazing knowledge of military and war machines," he thought.

As the kids stood there watching, an exceptionally tall man in a military uniform stepped off the helicopter and jogged towards the house. Grandma stepped through an opening in the wall and moved to him. We couldn't hear their conversation over the helicopter's whirling blades, but they only spoke for a moment. Then the man whose face was stern turned to the soldiers beside him and yelled, "Get them all to the base!"

As General Russell smiled at us, Malcolm took that time to examine him closely. He was a tall man, at least 6'6" tall, and he was black. There weren't many black generals. I looked at his shoulder and noticed four stars on it ... Wow! A four-star general! That's a big deal. He had to have been in the military a long time to have that rank. He did look old. He was probably 40 or 50 or maybe even older, but he was definitely old. He was clean-shaven with mahogany brown eyes that showed a lot of intelligence. I could tell he was absorbing as much information as he could as quickly as he could and trying to be friendly at the same time. When he spoke, his voice was deep, firm, and calm. I felt like I could trust him just from listening to his voice.

"Hi everyone," General Russell said. "We are going to get everyone to safety. The helicopter is set up to hold two ICU patients, and a full medical staff is onboard to immediately begin helping the injured."

Mom sniffed, and I saw that the medics were already working on Dad and Uncle Junior. "Can I ride with them?" she cried, interrupting the General.

"Of course, you can," the General said, looking toward Grandma who nodded her head, "but that only leaves one seat available on the helicopter."

Grandma spoke up then, "Yes! Let Cassandra travel with Junior and Aaron; I'll travel in the truck with the kids." She turned to Mom and spoke to her, "Cassandra, take care of my babies, and I'll take care of yours." They embraced tightly, and Grandma whispered, "I will protect them with my life."

The medics took Dad and Uncle Junior on gurneys towards the helicopter, and Grandma stepped between Mahalia and me, leading us through the jagged hole in the wall. The sky was streaked with the orange, blue, and brown hues of dusk, and the sun sank in the sky. "It will be dark soon," Olivia thought, as she watched Cassandra climbed behind them into the plane. In the yard, General Russell stood near an SUV that had arrived. Two soldiers stood at attention, listening to him. Mahalia and I just stood there with Grandma watching and feeling helpless.

"Olivia," General Russell said, turning back to us, "these soldiers will get you and the kids to the base. Go with them." Grandma nodded, and General Russell climbed aboard the aircraft and signaled the pilot to leave.

Mahalia looked at her grandmother, eyes wide, "Grandma where are they taking us?" She asked.

"They are taking you to an Air Force base. They will keep you safe."

Mahalia's eyes darted between Malcolm and their grandmother, "What do you mean, keep us safe! What about you? Aren't you coming with us, Grandma?"

"No," Grandma said, and I could tell she'd moved on. She had no intentions of traveling in a military SUV with Malcolm and me. She continued, confirming my suspicions, "I am going to get your grandfather. I must save Marshall."

"No Grandma! You have to go with us!" Mahalia snatched away from Malcolm and her grandmother, taking two steps back and balling her fist as she glared at her grandmother. "You have to be safe too! That crazy red guy could kill you! You are going with us!"

Olivia looked at her granddaughter, not finding the patience that she usually spared for her, and sighed, "Mahalia, this is not a debate. I am telling you to get in the truck and go with the soldiers to the Air Force base."

Mahalia's eyes watered, but she stood firm, "I will not! Not without you! You're always telling Malcolm and me to take care of the family! So, if you're going to get Grandpa, Malcolm and I are coming with you to help! You don't even know where he is and what are you going to do if Red Hood Weirdo catches you!"

Olivia sighed again, looking at her stubborn granddaughter, "First of all young lady, get yourself together. I don't care what's going on, YOU DO NOT TALK TO ME LIKE THAT, do you understand?" She glared at the girl, taking in her ruffled afro and firm set of her mouth. "She reminds me of Zena, Olivia thought, just as headstrong, just as beautiful."

"And secondly, I do know where your grandfather is! I have a tracker on him, your dad, your mom, and your Uncle Junior. And for that matter, I have a tracker on you and your brother too! I know where my family is always! And lastly, ma'am! There are so many things you don't know and don't understand. So, what I need you to do, and I need you to do it without argument or question, is to get in that SUV and go!" With that, Olivia took Malcolm and Mahalia's hands and guided them to the waiting truck. Malcolm hugged his grandmother tightly, told her he loved her, and slid into the cool interior.

Mahalia stood, with her head down, tears falling on her cheeks, and refusing to look at her grandmother. She would not talk back. She knew she'd gone too far before and that she needed to apologize for her sassiness, but right now she just couldn't. She was too scared.

Olivia saw that her granddaughter was struggling and knew in part it was because of how the family reared the kids. They had been told since they were babies to take care of the family. Now circumstances were not allowing the sweet girl to step up and do what she believed she should do. Olivia took her granddaughter's face into her hands and looked into her granddaughter's eyes. Softly she said, "For you to take care of the family now, I need you to get in the car and go to the base. I need you to watch over Malcolm on the ride and be strong for your mom, dad, and Uncle Junior when you get to the base. I love you, Mahalia. Go." She kissed the girl and gently nudged her to the truck. With unease, Mahalia slid into the truck and pulled her little brother close.

After standing in the yard, watching the truck until she could no longer see it, Olivia turned and sprang into action. Stepping into her private office, she picked up her phone and texted the one person she needed to help her husband, Zena, her daughter. The text was simple: **Oak Tree Down**, and she hit the send button.

"General Russell," a young officer turned to his commander, "the convoy with the kids is not responding. We've tried to reach them several times, and they aren't answering. And their GPS signal shows that they are stationary and have been so for the last 20 minutes."

The General looked at the soldier, his face brooding. "Are there drones nearby that can get us rapid visual intel on the situation?"

"Yes, sir."

"Get them out there now!" He ordered and added, "Let's get eyes on them, and then we'll determine how we should proceed. They may have stopped for food or bathroom."

Minutes later, the soldier summoned the General to a bank of screens. "The Bulldog Rising Drone has located the vehicle, and these are live images." On the screen, the General saw murky images of the SUV nose-first in a ditch. It was nighttime so the images were shadowy and dark, but even with that, the General could tell that the body of the vehicle was riddled with dents and dings. The windows were shattered and broken. "Deploy the Bulldog Microeye," the General ordered. "We need to see the inside of the vehicle."

The officer typed a series of commands on the keyboard, and the larger drone withdrew from the sight of the accident, rising several yards in the sky. When it was hidden in the trees, a latch on its underside opened, and a small bee-sized drone emerged. It quickly descended and entered the truck through a shattered window. New images filled the screen, and the General saw the two soldiers in the front seat. The tiny drone landed on the forehead of one of the soldiers, and his vital signs scrolled up the screen. The officer keyed in more commands, and the drone moved to examine the second soldier.

"Good," the General said. "They're both alive. Move the

Microeye to the backseat."

The drone entered the back of the truck, and nothing but black leather seats were visible. It moved to the cargo area behind the backseat; nothing was there either. "Have Bulldog Rising scan the area. Maybe the kids are hiding in the woods around the site."

The larger drone rose from its perch in the trees and moved through the area near the accident. It moved methodically, creating concentric outward circles of the radius of the accident. It navigated about half a mile away from the accident when the General noticed a huge scar in the landscape. There was a huge, jagged hole in the Earth, and it looked like something had plucked up a large tree. The root system which looked to be over 20-feet deep and wide had been snatched out of the Earth, leaving the Earth ripped and torn with broken roots pointed upwards and oozing sap. Interestingly, there was no tree laying on the ground. He knew some machines could pull a tree up by its roots, but there were no drag marks or tire treads. Whatever removed the tree had done so without disrupting the landscape around the tree.

"Get me still shots of the entire area and have the forensic team examine them. Send a team to get those men. When they are conscious, let me know. I need to speak to them. Figure out what happened to that tree!" the General instructed.

The General got up, moved down the hallway, and entered the medical facility. Looking through a glass wall, the General saw three beds. Each bed was occupied by a person. He sighed, as he watched nurses quietly adjust tubes on each patient. Aaron, Junior, and Cassandra lay on the beds. Aaron and Junior, in critical condition, healing slowly from the beatings they experienced, and Cassandra sedated due to the shock and stress of witnessing the whole attack.

The General ran his hand over his face. He had known Marshall and Olivia for years. They worked together on many missions, and he called them friends. This call would be difficult. Not only did he have to tell his friend and colleague that her kids were in critical condition, but he'd also have to let Olivia know her grandchildren were missing.

# Section 3

# The Plan

Sitting in the back of the military SUV with Mahalia's arm draped over his shoulders, Malcolm felt his eyes stinging with tears. He didn't want to cry. Grandpa would say that he needed to be strong, but it was hard because Grandpa had been taken away. Dad and Uncle Junior were hurt, and Grandma was alone. He felt helpless, and that made him want to cry. He was deep in thought and firmly trying to hold back tears when Mahalia leaned in towards his ear, "Malcolm, we have to go back and help Grandma, or she will die."

Startled out of his thought, he glanced up at his big sister. Her eyes were set. She had a plan. But he wasn't sure. "We are not supposed to use our powers outside the house." Malcolm insisted, still looking at Mahalia and realizing him saying that only made her more determined.

"You're going to do what I say little brother, or I'll use my powers on you!" She threatened, waving her hands, and creating a hologram image of Malcolm's video game console burning and all the file memory being deleted.

"Mahaila! Don't do that!" he whined.

"I will if you don't help me save Grandma! I can't do it alone, and I won't leave you behind!" Mahalia stared at her brother intensely, wiggling her eyebrows and frowning. "So, you'll do what I say so that we can help Grandma?"

Malcolm looked at the hologram. He knew, without a doubt, she could wipe his gaming history clean and cause the whole thing to overheat and burn.

He saw her do it when she wanted a new cell phone. She made her old cell phone mess up by using her powers. He thought Mom and Dad would have known, but they had no clue. She said, "Dad, my phone's not working," and looked at Dad so sweetly.

He had been working in his office for hours. At the sound of concern in her voice, Dad looked up from his computer and said, "Really? Bring it here." And that was when she did it. Sometimes Mom and Dad didn't notice when we used our powers. Maybe it was because they didn't have powers and didn't know what to look for. But I knew when Mahalia used her powers, and she knew when I used mine. We could always tell. She probably knew I had powers before Mom and Dad did.

She slid her fingers across the back of the phone, as she walked into Dad's office. I saw the tiny spark, and I saw her close her eyes for the briefest moment and sync with the phone's circuit board. I knew she had sent a small electrical surge to the circuit board. When she handed the phone to Dad, it powered on, but the images on the screen were distorted. Dad tinkered with it for a while, looking puzzled. "Did you drop in water or something?"

Mahalia looked up and said, "No Dad, it just started doing that." Knowing that if she'd dropped the phone in water or something like that, Dad would have been upset and called her irresponsible. She wasn't lying. The phone had just started doing that, but she left out the part about using her powers to help it along.

"Well, let me call the phone company and see what they say. It's weird that your phone just started acting up. But I'll see if I can get you a new one." Dad said shrugging his shoulders.

"Dad, since you're getting Mahalia a new phone, can I get one now. Please?" I asked. Mom and Dad didn't want me to get a cellphone until next year. They said that 5th grade was too young for a cell phone. But half my class had one, and with Mahalia busting hers on purpose, this would be her second phone.

"No, Malcolm," Dad said, "You know the rule: we'll see what your grades and behavior look like at midterm of 6th grade, and then we'll see if you have earned the privilege of a phone."

I sighed and looked a Mahalia who was grinning. "I waited until I was in 6th grade," she said. "I had all A's, and I only had had one detention that whole year."

"Yeah, Mahalia, I know you were perfect! Never do anything wrong!"

I started to tell on her for using her powers to break the phone, but I decided not to. She was my sister, and I didn't rat her out.

So now in the back of the military SUV with our family in trouble and some weird dude in a red nightgown shooting poison darts at them, I knew I had to do what she said. I nodded and said, "Ok Mahalia, I'll do it."

Mahalia laid out her plan to me quickly. "We are going back to help Grandma. I need you to hit the tires and blow them out with rocks. Then we'll run and escape."

I exhaled and looked at her not quite as certain of my powers as she was but said, "Okay, I'll try." I closed my eyes and did like Grandpa had been instructing me to do for years. I visualized the Earth—going from the large form of the Earth with oceans, mountains, rivers, deserts, and shores to smaller more specific objects, like boulders and sarsens. Then, I focused precisely on the rocks on the side of the road. I picture them in my mind. Quartz and granite pebbles—some small, some large. I zoned in on the large ones and visualize them rising and swirling. I keep them swirling, faster and faster. Then with my mind's eye, I hurl them forward and low, directed at the tires on the SUV. Suddenly, rocks started hitting the whole truck. I tried, but I wasn't as good as I wanted to be at moving the terrain thing. Humongous rocks crashed through the window, coming in from all directions. I heard the driver yell, and the other soldier groan as the rocks bombarded them.

"Malcolm!" Mahalia screeched, "Control it better!"

"I'm trying, but this isn't something I do all the time! I'm still learning!" I really did try to direct the path that rocks were coming in, but it just kept getting worse. More rocks flew at the car, and now they are all sizes—some as big as boulders, others as small as pellets.

I saw my sister's finger electrify; tiny sparks illuminated from her fingertips as she raised her hand to protect us from the spray of rock. Mahalia protected us with a force field. I heard air whirl out of the tires and felt the vehicle pulled into a swerve. The driver tried to correct the path of the truck but couldn't, so we skidded off the road. Both soldiers slumped forward in the truck.

"OMG! Malcolm! What did you do?" Mahalia gasped, looking at me.

"Ohhh no!" I scoffed. "You can't blame this on me! I did what you told me to do. You made me! I'm still learning how to use my powers. Grandpa has been training me! I did the best I could!"

The dust settled, and we looked at the soldiers in the front seat.

"You think they're dead?" I asked my sister, starting to feel bad about all the rocks. Their faces had been hit by several rocks, and blood oozed out of their cuts.

Mahalia climbed over the front seat and gently pulled the driver back, laying his head on the headrest. He moaned, and I sighed with relief. "No," she said. "They're not dead, but they'll be moving slow for a couple of days." She turned to the second solider and adjusted his head too. He moaned and tried to talk, and Mahalia climbed back into the back seat.

"Okay, let's get back to The Oaks." She said, opening the door and pulling me behind her. "We need to move fast before General Russell notices that we haven't made it to the base."

* * * * * * * * * *

General Russell sighed as he reflected on the state of Olivia's family. Cassandra had regained consciousness and was with her husband and brother-in-law. Both men were on the mend but remained asleep. He'd not told Cassandra about her children, and he was glad that she'd been so preoccupied with the men that she'd not asked. For now, he was off the hook from explaining to the woman that her children were missing. That would be short-lived. As soon as he walked back into the medical suite they occupied, he would have to tell her something about her children that would hopefully satisfy her. If he told her what he knew, it would not soothe her at all. He suspected that Cassandra would need to be sedated again when and if she heard the truth about her children's whereabouts.

He reached for the phone and dialed Olivia's number. This conversation was not one he looked forward to having. The team had gone to the location of the wreck and retrieved the two soldiers. Their injuries were minor, and when they'd been treated by the medical staff, he'd talked to them. The soldiers explained that Olivia had not gotten into the car with the children; she'd stayed at The Oaks. General Russell's face hardened with concern when he heard this. He'd heard Olivia when she said she was going to save Marshall. He tried to talk her out of a solo mission, and he'd hoped that Cassandra's plea for Olivia to travel with the kids would have persuaded her to wait for backup. But obviously, it hadn't.

The soldiers explained that both kids had been sitting in the back seat quietly talking when rocks and stones began spraying the car from every direction. They couldn't see the source of the pelting stones. The stones broke the SUV's windows and ruptured all its tires. The driver lost control of the SUV, and it had careened into the ditch. The force of the impact knocked both soldiers' unconscious because that was all they remembered about riding with the children. When they regained consciousness, the rescue team was there; the children had been gone, and they had no idea if they left on their own or if someone had taken them.

The forensic team made it to the site and found only two sets of footprints leading away from the wreck and to the location of the missing tree. The footprint trail stopped at the site of the missing tree. There was no evidence of anyone else being there. The footprints matched the approximate sizes of Malcolm and Mahalia's feet, but there was no other trace of their presence.

The phone rang. General Russell waited for the sound of Olivia's voice, but the answering service picked up instead. That caught him off guard. He took it to mean that Olivia had done exactly what he'd implored her not to do: left to search for Marshall, sending the children alone in the SUV. He didn't like the thought of her being on an unsupported mission, but her refusing to wait gave him no other option. Clearing his throat, he spoke to the answering service, "Olivia, this is Buford. There's been an occurrence. The car transporting the children was attacked, and the children are missing. I'll tell you more when you contact me." He hung up the phone and leaned back in his chair. Now, he must explain to Cassandra that her children and her mother-in-law were missing.

\* \* \* \* \* \* \* \* \* \*

Mahalia dragged me behind her, pulling me away from the scene of the wreck and toward the trees that line the edge of the road. "We can't let anyone see us!"

I looked around. The road we were on did not have a lot of traffic, but I knew eventually someone was going to ride by and see the truck with all the wheels blown out and the rock damage to the frame. Mahalia was right; we needed to hide until we figured out what to do. "What now, Mahalia?" I asked. I could hear the fear in my voice. She looked at me. I could tell she was trying to be brave.

"We've got to get back to The Oaks! We were only in the car about 10 minutes; we're not that far away."

I peeped through the trees at the wreck. "Mahalia, I don't think we can use the truck. The truck wheels are blown out."

"Yeah, I know! You did that Malc!" She grinned, looking proud. "And now I need you to do it again! You have to use your powers again and fly us to The Oaks."

This was just too much! This morning, I wasn't even supposed to use my powers unless Grandpa or Grandma were present. Now, this sister of mine wanted me to fly us home like it's as easy as playing Tetris. "How Mahalia?"

She scanned the area and then turned to me. "We'll find a tree and ride it to The Oaks. It's dark, so no one will see us." She said with a cool confidence that made it seem as though riding a tree was a piece of cake.

I was not as confident. I looked back at the wreck. "Can't we just drive the truck without wheels? Or can't you use your powers to fix the truck?"

"Nope, my powers won't work on that. Those are tires; they aren't electric. And what would you suggest we do with those two big dudes in the front seat: throw them in the ditch? That's not right Malc." She looked at me and continued. "You're our best chance. When the General and his team get here, they'll think Red Robe did this and go looking for him. They won't suspect us. We'll be back at The Oaks with Grandma, helping her save Grandpa! You can do this! Malcolm, you got this!"

Her enthusiasm was contagious, and I started to believe that I could do it. "Ok! Let's find a tree!" I shouted, and we began looking around for just the right tree. It was dark, but I could still tell how wide and tall the trees were. I knew the tree I needed had to be big.

"Let's use this one," I said, laying my hand on the trunk of a poplar tree that was about 60 feet tall and four feet wide.

Mahalia looked the tree up and down. "Wow, Malc! Are you sure you can do that?" Her eyes fell to the ground where she saw large roots anchoring the massive tree to the ground.

I was feeling myself now and chuckled to myself because of the confidence she had given me. "Didn't you see me bomb that truck with those rocks? I can do it! Just watch me!"

"Ok then! Let's do it!"

"Ok! Climb on up in the tree," I told Mahalia.

Mahalia settled on a thick limb and gripped it as tightly as she could. I wrapped my arms around the tree and closes my eyes.

For the third time that day, he focused on the Earth and all the things that it encompassed. With great effort, Malcolm channeled his energy and focused from the large to the small until his whole being became one with that tree. He wrapped his arms around the tree, pressing his face against the rough bark. The ground rumbled. Leaves scattered from the tree, and dust lifted from the ground as the tree ascended and began to fly. Mahalia scrambled to climb up the limb she was seated on. She grabbed and held on to the branch above Malcolm as the tree began to elevate and levitate turning from the vertical position into a horizontal plane.

"Eeeeehhhhh!" Mahalia squealed, clinging to the tree that bobbled and bounced in the air. Looking down, they saw dirt flying off the roots. They were about 10 feet above the ground. The roots trailed behind them, dragging on the ground. "Malcolm, go higher! The roots are dragging the ground! People will see us!"

Malcolm glared at his sister, momentarily losing focus. The leafy front of the tree tipped down, for just a second, and he quickly put his mind back to the job at hand, but he was still able to yell at his sister, "Mahalia! You're making me lose focus! Just hang on! Grandma will kill me if I tell her, you fell off the flying tree because I was using the powers I'm not supposed to use!"

The tree leveled out and moved smoothly now, about 35 feet above the ground. Both kids stood on the trunk of the tree, as the tree rose and leveled, horizontally. Malcolm was in control of the tree and held his palms out flat in front as a guide for the tree.

"Stay right above the road. It'll take us back to The Oaks" Mahalia yelled. Her afro fluffed in the wind, and she smiled, feeling exceptionally proud of her brother. They began to fly down the road. Zooming over the land headed back to their grandma's. She knew her grandma would not be happy about them coming back, but they had to protect the family. She looked at Malcolm and cheered him on, "You're doing great Malcolm!"

Malcolm smiled, amazed that he was able to keep the tree in the air and that he was able to steer it! He was starting to gloat a little but noticed the light coming towards them. No one could see them! What would they think? A flying tree being ridden by two kids. "Uggghhh!" He thought. "Mahalia, what's that coming towards us?"

Mahalia looked around her brother. "Ding dang it!" She blurted. "It's a car!" She scanned the earth beneath them and soothe her brother at the same time, saying, "Hey, just stay calm and move us over the trees, but don't stop!"

Moving them over the trees meant Malcolm had to elevate them at least another 20 feet. "I'm nervous." He said as he tipped his outstretched finger upward quickly. It was too quick. The whole tree jerked upward. Mahalia grabbed him around the waist, clinging to him to keep from being thrown off the tree. "Oh Nah!" Malcolm whispered. "Nah! Nah! NO!" He shifted his finger downwards. The tree took a huge dip, straight towards the road. Mahalia screamed, still wrapped around her brother, hanging on tightly.

In his ear, he heard his sister saying, "Don't hit the car! Keep us going and out of sight!"

"I'm trying! I'm trying!" He yelled back. Then he slowly raised his finger, and the tree rose slowly. "Yeahhhh boy," he thought, raising his palm just a little and being elated to see the tree gently rise, rather than lurch up.

His sister's grip around his waist loosened as they leveled back out. She said, "We are almost there! I see the gate of The Oaks!"

In the distance, Malcolm saw his grandparent's home. Warm yellow lights that were mounted on post throughout the yard illuminated the area. A wrought iron fence ran around the yard of the house and stopped at the stone columns that flanked the gate. In the center of the gate was the Robinson Family crest, a circle with intricate metalwork. The metalwork depicted the large oak tree with several limbs. One limb held the sun, while another held the moon. Below those limbs were other limbs— one clutched a lightning bolt and one with raindrops dripped off its end. Stars were being flung into the air off yet another large limb. All of these features were shrouded behind etched leaves that filled out the tree. Beneath the tree was a mighty stallion, with its main whipping in the wind, rearing upward, hooves high.

The large front yard covered at least two acres and boasted thick, green grass and shrubs near the house. "You've got to land this tree, Malcolm," Mahalia said.

"I know that," Malcolm thought, "but what I wasn't so sure about was exactly how to do it." My arms were still outstretched, and my palms were flat, parallel to the ground. I didn't want to point my fingers down because I knew that would cause us to nosedive into the ground. So, I lowered my arms and started to pull my finger back towards my palm, almost forming a fist. It seemed to be working. The tree began to slow down. And as it did, I also lowered my arms slowly. The tree began to descend, getting closer to the ground as I did.

"You're going too fast! Slow down! You're gonna crash into the house if you don't slow down!" Mahalia yelled. I did the only thing I could think to do. I closed my fists into two tight balls and dropped my arm to my sides. Not good. We lost all speed and began to drop straight down to the ground, fast! So, I raised my arm some and loosened my fist a little, but it was too late. We had already met the ground with a hard sliding thud. Mahalia flew over me and landed in the leaves and limbs of the tree, and I followed, tumbling, feet overhead, behind her. I heard Mahalia yelp when she landed, and I groaned. For a second, I just sat there, surrounded by the tree, and then I heard Mahalia calling out for me, "Malcolm, are you ok?"

Once I realized nothing hurt, I started pulling myself up through the branches and climbing out of the leaves. "Yeah, I'm ok," I said. "What about you?"

Mahalia had worked her way out of the tree and stood on the ground, looking around at the yard. "Boy, you messed up Grandma's yard. She gonna get you." She warned, glancing at the broken branches and scattering leaves that were strewn at least 15 yards across the lawn. Several large tracks of the lawn had been gouged up, exposing the creamy, white roots of the grass and the rich, silky blackness of the soil. One of Grandma's Cherokee climbing rose bushed that was attached to a six-foot trellis had been knocked over, and satiny red rose petals were everywhere.

"Mahalia! You made me do it! You're gonna be in trouble too!" I griped. "We'll be out here a week cleaning this up!" I said sadly, knowing the pride that my grandparents took in their yard.

We still were gawking at the destroyed lawn when a giant robot gorilla jumped out towards us. "What in the flipping fruity freaks!" Mahalia thought, and she quickly pushed her brother behind her. "What is this thing?" she wondered, looking at the huge robot that snorted and grunted circling them.

Malcolm pushed from behind Mahalia and looked at the robot closely. He was at least 10 feet tall, purple and red, with long powerful arms. His fists were metal, and his arms were made of what looked like silicon-covered galvanized metal. His vision plate showed at least 20 LED camera lights that glowed red and yellow. He moved towards us swiftly and aggressively. He stretched with each motion in an attempt to reach for us with his strong metallic hand.

"Stop! Do not move!" The gorilla said in an automated voice.

But we do move; we step away. Mahalia's hands glowed and electrified sparks popped off of them. She yelled, "You stop!" Mahalia pushed her sparkling hand toward the gorilla ready to tase him into a pile of scrap metal if needed.

toward the gorilla ready to tase him into a pile of scrap metal if needed.

Suddenly, Grandma appeared. She stood in front of us, looking at us, face firm and hand on her hips. The robot became motionless, his vision panel losing its amber glow.

"Malcolm! Mahalia! What are you doing here? Gibbs could have killed you both," Olivia scolded.

"Gibbs?" The kids say in unison, looking at their grandmother questioningly.

With a flourish, Olivia pointed to the robotic gorilla, "Gibbs!" she said. "But that's beside the point! Why are you here? I'm going to kill Russell! You are supposed to be safe at the base!"

"Grandma," Malcolm blurted, running towards his grandmother, and wrapping his arms around her waist. "Mahalia made me do it. She said she'd destroy my video game if I didn't, so I did. And I'm sorry about the yard. Grandpa didn't teach me how to land."

Olivia looked at her yard and took in the damage that her two lovely grandbabies had caused. Before she could say a word to them about that she heard her granddaughter explain what happened, talking a mile a minute.

"Shut up boy!" Mahalia started, pushing her way between Malcolm and her grandmother. "Grandma, I wasn't going to do anything to his game, but we couldn't let you do this alone. We had to come back and help you. So yes, I encouraged Malcolm to use some of his powers. And yes, we had a few difficulties landing. But we're here; we have powers. Please let us help!"

Olivia looked at both of them. "Wait. You flew a tree here? What happened to the soldiers who were taking you to the base?"

The kids looked at each other quickly. "There was an accident; they lost control of the truck. They got knocked out in the crash, but they'll be ok." Mahalia said.

Again, Olivia just looked at her grandchildren. "And the tree," she waved at the mass of leaves and branches all over the yard. "Did you fly a tree?" She pointedly looked at Malcolm who bashfully stepped away.

"Well, we don't have drivers' licenses for a car, Grandma!" Mahalia said. "And besides, all the tires on the truck got flattened in the crash." She added coyly.

"All the tires?" Olivia questioned still staring at her ten-year-old grandson, whose eyes would not meet hers. "It doesn't matter. And we'll deal with you two about not following directions later. You are not going to help in this rescue. In fact, I'm going to reactivate Gibbs and have him take both of you to a safe place because you're not completely trained."

Malcolm pipped in, "Aww ... come on Grandma! Please!"

Mahalia stomped. "But Grandma! We can do it!"

Using her hands, Olivia motioned a hard X in front of them, "Cut it! Do you two realize that there is a chance that I've lost two sons and a daughter-in-law today? My husband is being held captive and in danger, I'm sure. I can't lose you! I won't put you in harm's way."

Malcolm stepped up to his grandmother and took her hand. Looking at her, he spoke clearly and insistently, "Grandma, we are family. We must do this together. We were blessed with these powers for a purpose."

Mahalia stepped to the other side of her grandmother and hugged her tight, whispering in her ear. "Please Grandma, let us help you."

Sighing Olivia gave in, hugging her grandchildren tightly, saying, "Follow me." Before they turned towards the house, Mahalia's fingers began to spark. With a quick flick of her right wrist, she reactivated Gibbs and stared into his vision panel.

"There," she said, "I've synced into Mr. Gorilla Gibbs. He will do my bidding and protect us forever now."

Olivia smiled. She always knew that her granddaughter's ability to telepathically communicate with electrical systems would give her exceptional power in this modern world. "Mahalia, Gibbs is my robot. I control him." She said gently.

"No, Grams," Mahalia smiled. "He's our robot now, and we control him." She smiled sassily, and they entered the house.

Once in the house, the kids saw the shattered wall in the dining room, broken chairs, and rubble left from the attack. "This is serious," Mahalia thought as she glanced around the room remembering the soldiers and the Red Robed monster that had stormed their home just hours ago. "We got to show Grandma that we can help her."

Malcolm was thinking the same thing, and he spoke to his grandmother. "Grandma," he said, "we'll be stronger together!"

Olivia looked at her grandson and hoped he was ready for the battle that lay before them. Redirecting them from the dining room, Olivia said, "Come, children." She walked into the grand room.

It was decorated with heavy leather furniture and wooden end tables. A ceiling tall stone fireplace was on one side. Tall single-paned windows framed the fireplace and let light flood into the room by day. A wrought iron chandelier holding a series of bare lightbulbs from the 15-foot ceilings gave the room a warm glow in the evening. Directly across from the fireplace was a wooden wall. It seemed to be made of one solid piece of cherry wood that spanned the width of almost 30 feet of the room. In the center of that wall was the same crest that was on the gate. It was carved into the heavy wooden panels and polished to a high gloss. Rising almost six feet high, the crest was the central feature of the room. The kids had played in this room their whole lives and had run sticky fingers over the crest thousands of times, tracing the horse's mane and tail. When their grandmother stood in front of it and said to them, "Children hug me." They thought she was being sappy.

Malcolm asked, "What? Why?" He loved his grandma, but sometimes she was just way too mushy.

Mahalia sucked her teeth and crossed her arms over her chest, "Really Grandma, do we have time for this?"

Olivia shot both of them a hard look and said, "Just do what I say please."

They hug their grandma, and suddenly they felt the change. It was like the very molecules of the cells of their body were vaporized. But it didn't hurt. They just knew that the solidness of their being was no more. They were able to move through the minuscule openings in the wood, traveling to the other side of that wood. A side that they had never known existed.

That fragmentation of their solidness lasted only for a few seconds, and then they felt themselves normalize again, becoming solid once more. Flesh and blood. And they were in another place, still hugging Grandma tightly.

"Whooooaa!" Mahalia said touching her body to make sure she was solid. "What just happened?" She asked, fluffing her fro to make sure her springy curls would still spring after coming apart and coming back together so quickly.

Malcolm stepped away from his grandmother and looked around. "Wow! What is this place, Grandma?" He asked, looking at the equipment that included several huge walls sized high-definition screens, radars with red and green bleeping lights, and many computer panels.

"It's called The Roots," Olivia said smiling, looking immensely proud.

Mahalia was unimpressed. "Really, 'The Roots?' Like the bottom of a tree? That's so common, Grams. You and Grandpa could have been a little more creative. Like, say …," she looked around at all the equipment and keenly understanding the capabilities that were there, "Center Cosmos or Universal Center?"

Olivia smiled and shook her head, "No, it is not about the equipment or its capabilities. The Roots is about family. This is the place that our family has gone to for years to prepare, protect, plan, and commune. This place is your history and your legacy. Generations of powerful people have used this space to keep the world safe. The Roots speaks to our family's origins, Africa. It speaks to our family's core, love. It will provide you with a foundation of strength, bravery, and courage. The Roots, my loves, is where you will learn to draw what you need to defeat those that try to hurt you."

Mahalia looked at her grandmother and asked, "Then why didn't you ever tell us about this?"

Olivia smiled softly, pressed her hand together in front of her chest, and answered, "You didn't need to know. You are children, and children don't need to know grown folk's business. But anyway, now you need to know." Grandma said, turning around with her arm outstretched and face smiling, "Welcome to The Roots!"

Mahalia watched her grandmother and wondered who the 'powerful people' she'd talked about were. She shrugged her shoulders and thought grown-ups always talk about the past so seriously. She just didn't see the past as all that important, but Grandma and Grandpa always spoke about the past all mysteriously and stuff. She was still pondering the past when she saw movement behind her grandmother and brother.

Gliding across the clean gray marble floor was a robot. It coasted over to Grandma and stop in front of her.

"Mrs. Robinson," the robot stated, in a digitized voice that reminded her of her smartphone's voice assistant, "General Russell left a message for you." The screen on the robot's chest lights up, and the voice of General Russell streamed into the room. "Olivia, this is Buford. There's been an occurrence. The car transporting the children was attacked, and the children are missing. I'll tell you more when you contact me."

The message ended, and Mahalia looked at her grandmother who was working quietly at one on the computer panel, reviewing what looked like a GPS on the screen, with coordinates rolling over the satellite image of someplace on Earth. The robot stood next to her, unmoving and quiet. Grandma turned to the robot and ignoring the message General Russell had sent, she asked, "Did Zena reply?" I knew she was talking about our aunt, our grandparent's only daughter.

"You spoke to Auntie?" Mahalia asked, moving closer to her grandmother, and looking at all the screens that filled the wall. She liked Auntie Zena. She didn't see her often, but when she did, they always had a good time. She was pretty and wore great clothes. Auntie Zena told her that when she got older, they could go shopping for clothes, and she couldn't wait. Zena was cool.

"Yes, I contacted your aunt," Grandma said. She sounded sad, and that made the kids look at each other--remembering the reason they were here and all that had happened in the last 10 hours. "With everything going on she needed to know to make sure she stays alert and keeps herself safe."

"Is she still mad at Grandpa?" Malcolm asked. He knew that Auntie Zena and Grandpa were always arguing about how Zena used her powers. She never tried to hide them. She was like a superhero, and that upset Grandpa. He said that it made evil people draw to her which put her in unnecessary danger.

"Yes," Grandma sighed. "But she has to know what's going on. She has to protect herself." Grandma looked up distracted by the conversation that we were having, or maybe she was just worried. A lot was happening. "Grandma, you have another robot?" said Malcolm, smiling and walking over the robot, waving his hand in front of the lifeless hunk of metal and screens. The robot didn't respond.

Grandma glanced at Malcolm and smiled, turning in her swivel chair to face Malcolm and the robot. "Yes. His name is Douglass." Malcolm continued to try to get the robot to work, and Grandma didn't help him. Then Malcolm said, "Douglass!" Suddenly, the robot beeped and lit up.

"Mr. Malcolm, are you needing assistance?" The robot asked, and that delighted Malcolm. He grinned widely. He was trying to think of some spectacular command to give the robot, but Grandma stopped him before he put his idea in motion.

"No Douglass, he does not."

"Aww Grandma, come on!" Malcolm fussed, "I have a robot! Why can't I play with it?"

"Because you don't have a robot. I do, and it is not a toy. Right now, is not the time for that. When we get your grandfather home, I promise you, I will give you and Douglass ample time to get to know each other."

Malcolm didn't argue anymore. He knew that the job was to help Grandma find and save Grandpa.

"Grandma," Mahalia said, "where should we start to look for Grandpa?"

Grandma turned a looked at me, and I thought as I always did. She is so pretty. She was a chocolate brown woman with big, gentle almond-shaped eyes. She had full lush lips that she always coated in a pretty gloss, and she was fit too. Her legs were lean and strong. She didn't look like some of my friends' grandmothers. She didn't have loose arms or chubby thighs that needed hiding in ugly trousers. Her legs were defined and shapely. I hoped that when I got old like Grandma, I was as good-looking as she was.

"I know where he is already," Grandma said, with a cool smile on her face. "As I told you earlier, each family member has a location tracker. While those thugs were here, I was able to place a tracker on them too."

"Wait, what ... you put trackers on the Red Hood guy's soldiers when they were here?" Mahalia asked, looking in disbelief.

Grandma looked at me with a sneaky smile and nodded. "Remember, one of my powers is speed. I might have gotten a little slower with age, but I'm faster than them. And when they were here, I got a lot done! I placed tracers on them.

Grandma leaned back in the chair, crossed her arms, grinned, and nodded. "Dang Grandma! That's what I'm talking about!" Mahalia said, pumping her fist in the air. "So, what now? What do we do now?"

Olivia looked from her granddaughter to her grandson. She wasn't glad they escaped from the General's men, but their ability to pull off that escape let her know that they were ready for their inaugural mission. She would have to keep them close, but she was pretty sure they could handle themselves and even help if needed.

Answering her granddaughter, Olivia stood and calmly said, "Now we get ready to go save Marshall." Turning, she quickly gave orders to the robot, "Douglass activate the Red Tail One and prepare to leave."

Turning to her grandchildren, Olivia said, "We must rest before we go. We have been going nonstop since the attack." She led them down a hallway to a bedroom. "Douglass needs time to prepare Red Tail One, and I need to call General Russell to let him know you guys are safe. She continued, "You will rest I here, and I'll be next door." She pointed towards the bunk beds in the room. "There's a bathroom over there," she pointed. "Wash up, get some sleep, and I will be back to wake you when we're ready to leave." She kissed them both and left the room.

Soon Malcolm and Mahalia were in the bunk beds. Malcolm had chosen the top bunk. Mahalia lay, wide awake on the lower bunk.

"Malcolm, can you sleep?" Mahalia asked.

His face immediately popped down, hanging from the upper bunk, "No, I'm too excited to sleep." He grinned.

Mahalia laughed and agreed, "Me too little brother."

They eventually did fall asleep. And both dreamed of the adventure that lay ahead of them.

"Children, wake up," Olivia said, turning on the lights in the bedroom and walking to them. "It's time to go."

Malcolm sprang up and hopped off of the upper bunk, landing with a thud on the floor next to his grandmother. Mahalia swung her leg off the bed and stood quickly.

"Get cleaned up and come on," Olivia said, leaving them in the bedroom.

Both of the kids ran to the bathroom, brushed their teeth, and washed their faces, then followed their grandmother to the central room of The Roots.

Malcolm looked almost giddy. He hadn't believed Grandma would let them help. She was a grandma. Like other grandmas, she worried and told them to be careful. She insisted on placing a safety net on the trampoline and made him wear his helmet when he rode his bike. The fact that she was letting them go with her on the rescue mission excited Malcolm. And he wanted to show her that he was ready and could do the job more than anything. He was excited and eager when he burst out, "Hey Grandma! Are we getting suits? You know I like superheroes."

Grandma strode across the room, towards a large iron cabinet. The doors on the cabinet were black and heavy looking. When she reached it, a blue light ran the length of her face and back up. Then the wall talked, saying, "Olivia Robinson." Grandma replied, "AZM.20.17.17.06.15," and the heavy black door slid open.

Grandma investigated the opened cabinet and began to fill a black backpack with items, but she answered Malcolm's questions first. "No, I don't have anything in your size. You will keep on what you have. My plan won't have you near combat. You will do as I say and stay safe."

Even though Malcolm had committed to being mature and brave, Grandma's answer clearly was not what he wanted to hear. He stomped his foot, and mumbled, "Oh man, we don't ever get to do nothing fun!"

Mahalia agreed with her brother. She looked down at her outfit. "Really!?! My first mission and I'm wearing blue skinny jeans, sneakers, and a red hoodie. Boring!" she thought. "I'd look so good in a red-fitted catsuit with the family crest going down my left leg! But no, we don't get a suit! Dang!" She rolled her eyes, and she and her brother shared a disgruntle glance.

Grandma carefully placed round discs that glowed white at the center in the bag. She put a lot of them in the bag, and then she put what looked like a wand in a side sheath of the bag. Finally, she pulled out a small case and opened it up. Inside were numerous earbuds. She slipped a bud in one ear and left the other in the case, closed it, and dropped it in her bag. Zipping the bag up, she tossed it to Mahalia, who effortlessly caught it and put it over one shoulder.

Grandma walked with cool assuredness and crossed the room to stand in front of her grandchildren.

"Are you sure you guys are ready for this?" she asked, looking at them closely.

Malcolm smiled and nodded. Mahalia nodded and said, "Yes!" and their grandmother nodded to them.

Turning, they all looked at Douglass, who said, "The ship is ready Mrs. Robinson."

Grandma jogged toward the far side of The Roots. Another double door slid open, and Grandma yelled over her shoulder, "Children, let's go get your grandpa!"

# Section 4

# The Rescue

Together, they walked through the double doors that lead to a brightly light corridor. The children fell behind their grandmother, and Douglass glided beside them as they moved towards what looked like a landing pad for a rollercoaster ride. There they saw a glass-encased car with a smaller version of the family crest on its side. Illuminated electric blue, the interior of the car was made of black leather and chrome panels. In the center of the seats was a digitalized flat panel. Upon command, the doors to the car lifted like wings. Grandma stepped into the car and looked back at the kids. Their faces showed amazement. "Are you two coming?" she asked as Douglass glided through the opened door and locked himself into the car.

"Wow, Grams, what is this?" Mahalia asked stepping into the car. Malcolm ran to a seat, sat down, and began to touch everything. Douglass quietly explained to him how to use the digital panel. With only two or three taps on the screen, Malcolm had figure out how to adjust and harness himself into the seat.

"Oh, it's nothing special," Grandma smiled, "just the family concourse car. It makes getting to different parts of the compound easier. There's a whole series of tunnels under the compound, and this is one way we travel through them."

"One way?" Mahalia questioned. "What are the other ways?"

Olivia was amused by her granddaughter. If Marshall hadn't

been in so much danger, she would have loved to take her granddaughter on the definitive tour of The Oaks. The kids had so much to learn about their family. Yes, they knew they had powers, but the how and why of those powers had yet to be shared with her precious grandchildren. Marshall and she had always planned on telling them but not until they were a little older and had more control of those powers. The events of today suggested that maybe they should have started explaining more about the family sooner, rather than later. "Don't you remember? I can teleport you."

"Oh yeah, you can!" Mahalia smiled and nodded, once again charmed by her grandmother and all her powers.

"Grandma," Mahalia asked after they had been traveling for a few minutes. She had fallen somber as she thought about the day and all that had happened. She didn't give her grandmother a chance to answer before she continued, "Why did that man come after Grandpa?"

She paused and made eye contact with her grandmother, her face unsure and sad. Then she continued, "Is he really our grandfather?"

Olivia glanced at Malcolm and noticed him listening. There were so many things that she needed to tell her grandchildren, but time was not on her side. They were only minutes away from the Tiger's Den after leaving the compound. They needed to be focused on the mission, not the background story. Failure to focus could threaten their safety and lead to harm. Sighing, she looked at her granddaughter, "I don't know who that man was or why he's after our family. What I can tell you is this: your grandpa and I have done a lot of good and some terrible things with our powers. We have saved many, but along the way, some people were hurt. I guess that hooded man is one of the people we hurt." She paused and looked back and forth between her grandkids.

Malcolm spoke next. "And about what he said that he was our grandfather, mom's dad?" He questioned.

Olivia looked at her grandson. He still had a baby face, smooth and clear of blemishes and hair. He was just ten, with the same big eyes that his sister had, and her son Aaron's full pouting mouth. He had his dad's smile too. How could he be anyone's grandchild other than hers and Marshall's? Especially not that crazy psychopath's who burst into her home hours ago.

"Well," Olivia began, "I thought we knew everything about your mother, but things sometimes things aren't as clear as we want them to be." Almost talking to herself, Olivia continued, quietly. "We thought we'd checked everything. Everything! But I guess we didn't, or someone is lying about something."

Malcolm looked at his sister. Her brows were drawn, and her lips slightly parted. She looked as confused as he felt. But she didn't question their grandmother, so he followed her lead and remained quiet too.

The car came to a smooth stop, and the doors opened as everyone's harness lifted. The kids followed as their grandmother stepped out of the car. Malcolm looked around and realized with a jolt, "Grandma! We're underwater!" Olivia chuckled. "Why Malcolm, you are so observant!"

"Whatever," Mahalia teased, "he's not observant! He stated the obvious!" She touched the glass walls of the tubular walkway that their grandmother led them through. It was like being in an aquarium.

"Where are we Grandma?" Malcolm asked. He looked around and observed how the walkway opened to a large area. To the left were monitors with sepia-toned images. As he focused on the monitors, he saw that they were showing camera views of various places in The Oaks. There was the kitchen. Now, it was quiet, and he could still see the pots and pans Grandma had used to prepare their dinner. The screen flashed, and the front yard appeared. Gibbs, the gorilla, was walking around the yard, hacking up the transport tree into big hunks with his powerful fists. The garden flashed on the screen next, and Malcolm smiled when he saw the mound of dirt Grandpa had moved with Uncle Junior on it. His smile faded. Uncle Junior and Dad were hurt. Faintly, he wished he'd resisted his grandmother's instruction and gone to the base. At least that way he'd be closer to his mom and dad.

He was drawn out of his melancholy by his grandmother's voice. "This is the Tiger's Den," she said. "It's the transportation hub for The Oaks."

Now Malcolm noticed that there were motor vehicles of all sorts lined up on the other side of the room. Malcolm saw motorcycles, small four-wheelers, and other off-road vehicles.

"Wow! Grandma! When do I get to ride these?"

"Malcolm, when you get older, you'll get your chance." He ran to the vehicles and slid his hand over the shiny chrome of one of the motorcycles, noticing that it had a screen and control panel.

"Grandma, you and Grandpa ride?"

"We did, back in our active days ... we did a lot of things you don't know about. Now be careful touching those   ...   those are not your ordinary old road vehicles. Most are one-of-a-kind prototypes." She smiled steering Malcolm away, "You press the wrong button on one of those babies, you might detonate a bomb."

Malcolm's hand jerked back, and he looked at his grandmother with his mouth in an O. "Really! Grandma!"

"Well, perhaps not a bomb," Olivia said tilting her head with a smirk on her face, "but let's use caution anyway," she said as she gently pushed her grandson away from the vehicles.

Mahalia watched her brother and grandmother move back toward the center of the room. Then she noticed the right side of the room. There she saw the digital guts of something that looked like a huge tiger. She moved toward the circuit boards and hard drives. She felt her fingertips tingle, and then the codes and programs of the strange apparatus flowed through her mind.

Olivia noticed her granddaughter seamlessly integrating with the computer system. Even though it was not completely developed, she saw that Mahalia had begun to communicate with it. "Mahalia," she called to her granddaughter. "The system's not complete yet."

Mahalia's eyes were centered on the system, but she replied, "I can tell, but Grandma, there's so much information here! So much I want to learn."

"I know you do, but now's not the time." Olivia said, "You'll have time later, after your grandfather's home and safe."

Mahalia disengaged herself from the circuitry and looked at her grandmother. "You're right." She said and walked to her grandmother.

Olivia stepped in front of a screen that showed the world broken down into a large electrical coordinate plane. The screen wasn't that large, about 24 inches wide and 18 inches tall. On it, Mahalia noticed, eight points highlighted by blinking yellow lights. On the side of the screen, she noticed each member of her family's names scrolling with coordinate points next to them. Three of the coordinate points were the same (30.898315, -81.420994). Mahalia studied the screen more closely. "That must be Mom, Dad, and Uncle Junior at the base Grandma had wanted us to go to," she thought. Then she noticed that her grandma, Malcolm, and she had the same coordinate points, and she saw that the point was highlighted on the screen with a small icon of a tree, The Oaks. She saw Auntie Zena's location, and then she saw Grandpa's location (29.0698, -90.4963). She looked up to her grandmother and pointed to the screen. "That's where Grandpa is?" She questioned. Her grandmother's face hardened, and she nodded.

"That's where he's at," Olivia replied. She turned and looked toward the far side of the large room and began walking, "And that's where we're going," she said.

She had walked about 20 yards in about two seconds, not realizing that in her anxious state she'd begun to use her super speed, leaving her grandkids chasing after her. When they caught up with her, Malcolm was once again filled with awe and amazement.

"A spaceship! Grandma! This is brilliant!" Malcolm announced, reaching out to touch. "Why didn't you tell me sooner!"

His delight tickled Olivia. She smiled and watched him examine the vehicle, saying, "Well, technically it's not a spaceship. It's actually an amphibious hovercraft. The family's hovercraft. We call it Red Tiger 1. Now, let's go."

Turning to Douglass, Olivia nodded, and Douglass glided over to the craft and connected with it by placing his digital hand over a panel. The craft's doors slid open, and Douglass entered. He immediately moved one side of the vehicle and began working. Olivia and the kids entered the craft. Olivia motioned for Malcolm and Mahalia to sit in the two chairs that were behind the cockpit. "Mahalia," she said, "you will need to watch the companion panel and take quick notes on how to fly this thing."

They noticed that Douglass had opened the forward wall of the Tiger's Den and revealed a tight launch tube. Like the entry walkway, they could see the water outside the tube. But this tube was directed upwards.

Mahalia looked at her grandmother nervously. "I can fly the ship with my powers?" She then glanced at Douglass.

Olivia barely looked up, confident in her granddaughter's abilities. "Douglass," she said, "show her how the companion controls work. When we get to our destination, I will need you with me, and she can manage the ship on her own."

"Yes, Mrs. Robinson," Douglass said, gliding toward Mahalia and quickly instructing her on the use of the controls that mirrored a flight simulator.

Mahalia was listening but noticed that the craft had begun to move through the launch tube. "This mission was happening," she nervously thought, as Douglass continued to show her the controls. Her grandmother spoke to her now, giving more direction for the mission. "Mahalia, you will need to synchronize with the craft's system and keep up with the new data and intel it gathers. Correlate it to the Oak's system to make sure that we're always in safe water and airways. If you detect anything that might hurt us or anything you are not sure of, tell me or Douglass."

Olivia took the book bag she had given Mahalia when they'd left The Roots off the girl's shoulders. Opening it, she retrieved a second earbud from the case and placed it deep into her granddaughter's ear. "This will give you real-time data on me and my location and surroundings. It will also allow you to remain in contact with me. No matter what, do not remove it!" Olivia turned to Malcolm and placed a third earbud in his ear.

Mahalia nodded as she allowed her being to be drawn completely into Red Tiger 1's computer system. She'd never had so much binary information racing into her! It was exhilarating! There was so much information. She noticed that the craft's system was able to enter the military's system, but that there was no corollary relationship. The military could not enter Red Tiger 1's system.

"We are about 20 minutes from the target," Douglass announced. Looking out of the craft, Mahalia saw that the sun had risen. Grandpa had been gone almost 24 hours. She prayed he was still ok.

"Mahalia, have you figured it out? Can you handle the craft?" Olivia didn't even bother to look at her granddaughter because she knew that Mahalia was quite capable of handling the craft.

"Yeah, Grandma, I've got it," Mahalia replied. She'd combined Red Tail 1's and the military's mainframes and projected a hologram of the information in front of her face. She had also created a hologram of the stereoscopic projection of the location of the coordinates for her grandfather. Looking at the glowing images that only she could see, Mahalia realized that her grandfather was on Timbalier Island. She focused on the island and retrieved information about it through her connection to the Internet. "Grandma, I think he's on Timbalier Island. It's a barrier island that has an old oil refinery on it. The government put it out of commission years ago, but the structure is still there. It's on the southeastern coast of Louisiana. Grandma, if Grandpa is on Timbalier's Island, he's there alone. The government says that the island is disappearing due to erosion, All the people moved away a long time ago. No one's there," Mahalia said talking to her grandmother.

"Is that what your computer sense is telling you?" Olivia asked her granddaughter.

"Yes."

"But your grandfather's tracker is active and sending signals. So, someone is there. Do you detect any computer processing coming from the island?"

With her mind, Mahalia opened another hologram screen and scanned the area for Wi-Fi, Bluetooth, or any binary signals. If the island was truly uninhabited, there would be no signal. But she immediately felt a Wi-Fi signal. Realizing that if there was a Wi-Fi signal coming from where her grandfather was, there may also be radar that could detect them, Mahalia created a firewall around the craft and blocked digital detection of the craft and the computer systems she had tapped into.

"Grandma, the island has a Wi-Fi signal, so I doubt that it's uninhabited."

"Yes, but whoever's there doesn't want us to know they're there," Olivia said looking out of the window. They were flying over the Gulf of Mexico and near the coast of Louisiana. There was lots of murky water, and she could see where the water of the Mississippi River rinsed into the Gulf of Mexico.

She moved out of her seat and stood between Malcolm and Mahalia. "Listen, kids. Soon we'll descend and have an aquatic landing. Mahalia, as soon as we land, I'll disembark and follow your grandfather's tracking signal to find him. Douglass will travel on land with me. Once we are off the craft, you put Red Tail 1 back in the air. Keep the firewall up and the radar blocker on. Circle the area and listen for further instruction. Douglass will let you guys know what we need."

Feeling left out, Malcolm slumped in his seat. "Grams, what do I do?" he whined.

She turned to her grandson and noticed his pout. "Malcolm, if the Red Hooded guy is here, his soldiers will be here too. They will have their tranquilizer darts. Although I am wearing my uniform now, and the darts shouldn't be able to penetrate it, the soldiers are still a threat. I need you to listen. When I tell you, use your powers."

She took his hand and led him to a numeric panel on the wall. "Type in your birthday," Olivia said. Malcolm carefully typed 08072011. A panel on the side of the craft slid upwards from the floor. He heard a hum and the foil board slipped out of the panel.

"A foil board?" Malcolm said, reaching down and picking up the three-foot-long silver and blue board. It was surprisingly light, but Malcolm wasn't impressed. "Grandma, you want me to surf while you, Douglass, and Mahalia rescue Grandpa?" He cocked his head to the side and looked at his grandmother, starting to feel like she wanted to leave him out of the adventure.

"No, son," Grandma corrected. "This is not a regular foil board. Do you see a tube for water?"

Malcolm flipped the board over and looked. "No, so how does it work?" He'd been hydro foiling since he was little. With his grandfather being able to manipulate water, the family would often go to the beach. Grandpa had created a hydrofoil effect for him, allowing him to ride the waves without a board. When it was just Mom, Dad, Mahalia, and him, Dad paid for hydro foiling for the family. He loved it and was great at it, but on a regular hydrofoil, a tube pumped in the water, and you had to be able to balance on the board as the water lifted you several yards in the air.

"It works on wind and air, Malcolm. You've been training to do this since you were small. As Douglass and I send you instructions, you will travel on the foil and use your powers of the Earth to stop the soldiers. Your job is so important. You must keep them so busy that they can't stop us from saving your grandfather." Olivia paused and looked at her grandson. She noticed that although she told him to wash up this morning, his curly brown hair still had tree debris in it, and his face was still smudged with dirt from the tree flight. He looked very young and very frightened.

"Well, umm, Grams," he started, "that's a lot. What if I fall off the foil?"

"You won't," Olivia said simply, confident in his abilities. "You've worked with your grandfather on this for years. You know how to do this."

He swallowed and sighed. "But Grams, I don't want to hurt anybody." He lowered his head.

"Just slow them down; you don't have to hurt them. We need you, Malcolm. Ok?"

Malcolm looked up. His grandmother was looking at him, and he heard his grandfather's voice in his mind, "Protect the family." And he nodded, "Ok, I can do it."

Olivia turned to Douglass. "Ok Douglass, let go. Mahalia, land on the water, and I'm going in to get your grandpa. And kids, if Douglass orders to you leave, you are to immediately leave. Do not come after me! If I can't get your grandfather out, you are to find General Russell and your parents. If Douglass tells you to abort the mission, take the craft and go to the base."

"Grandma, we are not leaving you," Malcolm quietly said.

"No, we won't!" Mahalia said defiantly.

Olivia looked at her grandchildren—Mahalia, who effortlessly controlled the craft, frowning up against the idea of abandoning the mission for any reason, and Malcolm, who looked worried and concerned, clutching the foil board. "Children, I plan to come back with my husband. I do not plan to leave without him. But if things go bad, or if you are in danger, I need you to leave! I promised your mother that I'd make sure you were safe. And since you guys decided not to follow directions and go to the base …" She held up her hand, saying, "I'm certain you two had something to do with that wreck." She let her eyes move between her grandchildren. Their lowered eyes told her that she'd struck on the truth. "Like I said," Grandma continued, "if Douglass or I tell you to leave, you are to leave! Mahalia, the craft is programed with coordinates of the base, as I'm sure you're already aware of, and General Russell will know what to do. Do you two understand?"

They both nodded.

"Ok, Mahalia, land on the water in the marsh," Olivia said.

Mahalia eased the craft onto the water. It landed quietly and glazed across the greenish-gray surface of the swampy water. Looking out the window, she saw lots of animals. Among them were also alligators, turtles, and snakes laying around in the early morning sun warming themselves. She figured there were fish and other animals in the reed and bush that grew thickly in the swampy water. Peering out the window, she saw a large metal-framed building surrounded by a few silo-looking buildings. There were also large reservoir tanks and a simple system of roads that connected about 15 smaller buildings with them.

Grandma whizzed onto the island, while Douglass utilized his ski propulsion to glide across a wave onto the shore.

"Mahalia," Grandma chimed in her ear, "can you enter the island computer system?

Mahalia focused but found that she was unable to connect with any system on the island. "No, Grandma, but there has to be a system. I detect the Wi-Fi."

"Douglass," Grandma said, "are you in the facility?"
"Yes, Mrs. Robinson, I am."

"Find the system, Douglass. We need to know who we are dealing with and where they are. Mahalia, you have access to Douglass' system. When he connects on the hard frame, you will have access to everything. But for now, get the craft back in the air."

Mahalia nodded, and steered the craft back into open water, increasing speed steadily until the craft lifted off the water and sailed into the sky.

Olivia crouched down low in the abandoned entryway. Reaching into her bag, she pulled out a PBunnion and attached it to the wall of the booth that was connected to the main building. A PBunnion was an explosive that sent out a piercing sound wave. PBunnions could be remotely detonated, and the operator has the option of detonating the explosive, the sound wave, or both. PBunnions were small, no larger than a golf ball, and were able to automatically camouflage, taking on the color and texture of their

surroundings so that they were imperceptible. She planned to plant these along her path and detonate them as needed to impede any soldiers that got near her.

"Mrs. Robinson. Mahalia. I'm connected." Douglass said.

Mahalia didn't have to do a thing. As soon as Douglass connected to the facility's system. Another informational hologram opened before her. She glanced at Malcolm, who was once again seated next to her, and marveled that only she could see the information from the computer.

"Ok Grandma, I see the signal from Grandpa's tracker. I see the layout of the facility too. Grandpa is in one of the buildings in the center of the facility, on one of the upper floors. You are at the northmost entrance of the facility. Grandpa is southeast of you. You must walk through the main building, go east, and enter the Reservoir Room. Once you get there, you have to figure out how to get to the upper floor. There are stairs, an elevator, and a service lift. I can't tell if it's safe because the old cameras don't work."

Mahalia monitored the holograms so closely that she had not noticed anyone enter. But hearing her brother say, "Auntie!" she turned and saw her Aunt Zena coming through the teleport tunnel on the back of the craft. She had never been so happy to see her aunt. Her reddish-brown hair was as stylish as ever, and she looked great.

Walking up to the control panel, Zena said, "Hey kiddos! Where's my mom?"

Mahalia and Malcolm both began to talk at once, sharing the plan for rescue and the location of their grandmother.

Zena didn't interrupt them or admonish them for talking over each other. She listened and put together the pieces. "Ok, so Mom's inside the facility with Douglass." Both children bobbed their heads up and down. "So, we just have to wait for instructions." Again, the kids bobbed their heads as she eased into one of the pilot seats. "Ok then, troops! We wait!" Zena said, feeling pleased to see how well her niece and nephew were handling their first mission.

Olivia crept along the facility's exterior walls, planting PBunnions as she went. They immediately looked like the silver siding or shiny window that she applied them to. When she found her husband, she planned to level this place, and the PBunnions would do the job. When she had planted several of the PBunnions along the outer perimeter of the facility, she returned to the north entrance and tried to open the door. Surprisingly, it was unlocked. Using her lightning speed, she whizzed across the main floor and hid in a hallway with recessed doorways. Peeking around the corner, she saw that the main building had been converted to some type of command post. A soldier dressed in the same way that her family's attackers had been dressed looked at computer screens and panels. They worked quietly, and no one noticed her. Using all her speed, she whizzed around the room moving, stealthily planting PBunnions and heading east, towards the Reservoir Room.

Reaching the Reservoir Room, Olivia understood why it had that name. This must have been where oil from the old refinery was stored long ago. It had been cleared and cleaned of all crude oil. There were long pipes that ran across the room. Each of the pipes was at least 12 inches in diameter, and some were larger. On several of the pipes, there were large drums that once held chemicals used to clean crude oil. Now, Olivia noticed these pipes and drums had been retrofitted to hold guns, tasers, and ammo. Bazookas were attached to other pipes, and missile heads were everywhere. She also noticed several hundred cases of neatly lined-up darts. Olivia planted dozens of PBunnions in the Reservoir Room. The explosion would be magnificent, she thought. Looking around she saw that all the pipes in the Reservoir Room lead to a huge multi-story silo-like structure.

"Mahalia," she whispered, standing at the base of the silo. "How close am I to your grandfather?"

Mahalia looked at the hologram that floated before her face of her grandparents' locations and realized that her grandmother was standing about 50 feet below her grandfather. Her heart raced, and she felt her palms tingled. "Grandma, you're right below him! He is above you. Grandma, you don't see him?"

"He must be in this silo thing. I'm standing at its base. Look, Mahalia, I need you to create a distraction. Fly the craft across the front of the facility and fire. And I mean FIRE!"

"Grandma," Mahalia screeched, "I don't want to kill nobody!"

"And I don't want you to kill anyone. But I need all the soldiers to head out front. Malcolm, it's your time! When your sister draws the soldiers out, you shake and bake 'em! Ok?"

Malcolm's eyes were so big that Mahalia thought they'd pop out his head. And he didn't answer his grandmother; he simply nodded his head rapidly. He stood up quickly and clutched the foil to his chest, still nodding. He moved toward the panel that the foil had come from. There, ready at the flip of a switch, was a launching pad that would send him on the foil to move the Earth.

"When you want me to do it, Grandma?" Mahalia asked.

"Get into position now! And wait for my signal. When I count down to zero, you fire and do not stop until I tell you to. Just spray the front of the facility, keep circling and firing some more."

"Grandma! What if they shoot at me or Malcolm?" Mahalia asked in a panic.

"Mahalia, the craft can handle most military-style bullet shots. If you are ever in danger of craft failure, Douglass will tell you. You are then to get Malcolm, retreat, and go back to the base.

Malcolm, remember what your grandfather has taught you! You stay in the clouds, and they won't see you. Now we've got to get moving. Mahalia, are you in position?"

"Yes, Grandma, I'm ready," Mahalia said confidently.

"When I get to zero, you get started!"

Mahalia lined the crafted up and locked the firing heads into position, aiming for an area of about seven feet from the facility. All she had to do was wait for her grandmother's signal to hit fire, and hundreds of bullets would spray down on the grounds of the facility.

"Malcolm," Zena said, "get out on the launcher."

But when they looked over to Malcolm, they saw that he was frozen with fear. Tears poured out his eyes, and he hung his head low with shame.

Mahalia was not sympathetic. "Malcolm!" She yelled. "Get your butt on that launcher and fight before I come kill you myself!" Mahalia hissed.

"I can't! I can't!" Malcolm wailed, clutching the air foil to his chest.

"Mahalia, you do you!" Zena snapped, heading toward Malcolm. "I got Malcolm."

Suddenly, Olivia started a slow count down. "Five.... Four....

Zena kneeled in front of Malcolm, "Come on kid. You can do this," she coaxed. I'll head back to my ship, and I'll be fighting with you and helping you." She heard Olivia make it to the number two on the count down. Without waiting for an answer from Malcolm, she grasped his hand, and together they entered the launching pad. Knowing that her father had trained him well, she grabbed the foil from him and gently pushed him off the launching pad. Hearing the number zero behind her, she jumped too, releasing the foil. It quickly did what it was designed to do. It scooped through the air and glided under Malcolm. When his feet landed, they easily maneuvered it through the air and sailed into a fluffy tuft of clouds, just as Zena had predicted. As she glided through the air behind him, Zena watched her nephew quickly acclimate to sailing and surfing the air like he had been doing on water since he was two.

She smiled and summoned her aircraft, Lady J, and slid through the transport launcher. Quickly moving to the control panel, she turned the craft sharply and headed towards the sound of hundreds of bullets being fired. She whipped the craft above Mahalia's craft and surveyed the action below. Soldiers were pouring out of the facility and firing towards Red Tail 1. Turning hard, she traveled to the back of the facility and began firing just like her niece, drawing soldiers towards her.

Malcolm quickly adjusted to the foil and realized he was prepared. He glided and switched, zooming left and then right through the clouds until he found just the right spot that he could hover over the action below. Mahalia fired across the front of the facility, and Auntie Zena fired across the back of it. The soldiers were outside firing back. Malcolm surveyed the area and focused as hard as he could on the Earth below. The ground slowly began to buckle upwards. Soldiers toppled, their guns flying. Waving one hand out toward the soldiers, Malcolm created a series of three-foot ripples in the terrain under them. He laughed as he watched them fly upwards and crash back down to the Earth. With his other hand, he lifted the swamp water and hurled it toward the soldiers who were firing at Auntie Zena. The animals that lived in the water went with it. Malcolm was delighted to see swamp water filled with alligators, crabs, and snakes rain down on soldiers. He felt triumph as he watched soldiers running away from alligators, and crabs clamping their claws onto other soldiers' legs.

Inside, Olivia heard the commotion and quickly zoomed up the staircase stopping on the upper level. The room was large. Olivia heard the soldiers in the room yelling, "She's here! It's her! It's Olivia!" They said, running toward the window. "They're firing on us! On both sides!"

In the room, Marshall lay strapped to a metal slab. His arms were bound with metal restraints at the wrist and elbow. His legs were similarly restrained. Around his neck was a metal collar. It hurt Olivia's heart to see her husband tied down like that. She quickly stepped into the room and saw the Red Hooded man standing, looking out the window.

He spoke but didn't turn to face her. "Olivia, so glad you could make it," he said. Olivia reached for Bo Staff. The weapon unfurled at her touch, stretched out six feet, and glowed with white lights at each end. She took her stance, prepared to attack this man. As she did, soldiers approached, creating a barrier with their bodies around the man in the Red Hood.

"Man up!" She said. "Tell your soldiers to get out of the way and fight me or I will kill them," Olivia said, stepping toward the soldiers determined to settle things with the mad man who had wreaked havoc on her family and held her husband.

The soldiers tightened their circle and began their assault on Olivia. The first soldier aimed his gun and shot tranquilizer darts at Olivia, but unlike at the house, Olivia was dressed in her protective uniform that could easily withstand the darts. They ricochet off her, scattering around the room. Olivia used her Bo Staff and swiped the room sending one of the soldiers flying. The laser tip of the Bo Staff emitted a plasma wave at another soldier. It hit him in the chest and sent him flying backward, slamming into the wall of the room, and sliding to the floor. Using her super speed, Olivia duck and missed a blow the third and largest soldier

tried to land. He was massive, at least seven feet tall, and well over 300 pounds, all muscle. Dashing swiftly, Olivia retracted and anchored her sword, moved behind the giant soldier, and landed a blow on the back of his neck. The blow only slowed him, and she noticed the remaining soldiers approaching her. Once again, removing her sword, she moved, turning her super speed up to the point where they could not see her. They only saw the ring of static electricity her speed caused as the particle of air became charged due to her enormous kinetic energy that moved electrons away from their atoms.

As she circled the soldiers, Olivia created a plasma noose around the bodies of the soldiers, tying them together in a sizzling rope of plasma. She knew the plasma seared into their flesh. Their wails were loud and shrilling. Olivia released them, letting them crash to the floor as she moved towards her husband.

"Very good, Olivia. That was excellent fighting." The Hooded Man said, turning and holding one of his fists towards Olivia. When he suddenly extended his arm, a flash of light expelled from his bracelets. The light was a stun ray. When it hit Olivia, even her uniform could not stop it. The air was knocked from her lungs, and she was tossed backward across the room. Landing on her back, Olivia tried to move, but the hooded villain kept the stun ray aimed at her, immobilizing her.

"Who are you?" Olivia croaked.

Hooded Man smiled and pushed his hood back. He was a white man with cool blue eyes. His straight nose framed a sinister smirk that stretched between thin pink lips. His hair was graying, but the mostly brownish blonde hair was still thick. He released a small chuckle and said, "My brother's keeper, Olivia." Still shocked and held in place by the stun ray, Olivia looked at this white man in disbelief. His smirky smile grew as he continued, "Yes, Marshall and I are brothers. He didn't tell you about me."

He paused and let his eyes moved to his brother. "Shame on you Marshall, not telling your wife about your brother." Returning his glaze to Olivia, he rasped, "I'm his older brother. My name is Titus. I thought you may want to know my name before I kill you."

Olivia was still unable to move, but she was able to see her husband, still strapped to the metal slab across the room. He pulled against the metal restraints, his super strength causing them to buckle. The restraints gave off a charge that struck Marshall in the chest. He jerked at the shock and momentarily stopped pulling at the restraints. He had been taking those charges for the last several hours and being injected with the tranquilizing drugs that had laced the darts, but he still fought to get out of the metal straps that held him captive. They were made of a magnesium and tungsten alloy that was fortified with pure chromium and woven together with ultra-high molecular weight polyethylene fibers, resulting in a material that was flexible and so strong that it could not be broken by Marshall in his weakened state.

Her husband had never mentioned a brother. She knew that he had been born with a twin sister, who died when they were babies, but never any mention of a brother.

"Some brother you are!" Olivia said. "Brothers don't hurt and destroy each other! Holding down your brother's wife and injuring his kids! You are nothing! You are a coward." Olivia yelled.

"Oh, but I have my reasons for this," Titus said, looking at his brother. "My family hasn't always treated me in a familial way. Marshall, you told your beautiful wife nothing of the life we've lived. I'm surprised."

"Let us go!" Olivia yelled.

"Can't do that," Titus said. "Too much unfinished family business. I'll take care of you first and then move on to the rest of the family."

Mahalia sat up in the craft, shocked and scared. She listened to her grandmother and who she assumed was the Hood Man argue. He had said he was Grandpa's brother, but he was hurting her grandparents right now. She had to help! "Malcolm! Aunt Zena!" she yelled into the craft's radio, "Grandma and Grandpa need your help." She waved her hands, and the GPS coordinates of their grandparents' exact location were transferred to Malcolm's foil and Lady J

"Got it!" Zena said. "I'm on my way!"

The foil that Malcolm glided on shifted and turned in the direction of that the coordinates provided. With the grace of an experienced foil rider, Malcolm held his hands aimed at the ground and continued to create chaos on the ground below the soldiers but moved toward the location of his grandparents.

"Malcolm," Auntie Zena said, "Keep doing what you're doing! I'll get my parents."

Zena set Lady J into auto mode, slid through the launcher, and propelled herself through the window of the room that her parents and this maniac were in.

Landing smoothly between her mother and Titus, Zena waved her arms upwards. Fire erupted from her right hand and struck Titus in the face. The red hood burst into flames. "Get off of my mother," she yelled, using her left hand to create a frosty frozen mound of ice around his feet. His hand dropped, and the stun ray that had capture Olivia dissipated.

Olivia quickly recovered and began to move to the controls that operated the restraints holding her husband. She disabled the charger that sent electrical shocks through her husband's body and disengaged the restraints. With a hum and a click, the restraints lifted, and Marshall was free.

Although he was weak, he was able to move to his wife. Olivia embraced her husband and looked at him. "We have to get you out of here," she said, turning to her daughter. "Zena, we must go!"

Zena turned and looked at her parents. Her mother supported her father and whizzed toward the Zena. They embraced, and Olivia teleported them back to Red Tail. Olivia said, "I'll detonate the PBunnions and bring this place to the ground!"

"Douglass, you have 20 seconds to get out of there!" Olivia yelled, taking out the small, detonation device that controlled the PBunnions she planted throughout the facility. She set all the PBunnions to explosion mode with a 10-second shock wave delay. The explosion would destroy the facility, and the shock wave would further halt the soldiers' pursuit of them.

"Yes, Mrs. Robinson. I'm on the retreat!" Douglass said, detaching himself from the facility's hard drive and flying towards Red Tail 1.

"Mahalia," Olivia yelled into the headset, "store all the data you retrieved from this godforsaken place on The Roots system. We'll analyze it later."

"Yes, Grandma!" Mahalia replied.

"Malcolm, get back to Red Tail 1," Olivia ordered.

Malcolm heard his grandmother and lowered his hands. The ground that he had been manipulating fell suddenly still causing the few soldiers left fighting to fall to the ground. He turned the foil and calmly maneuvered it back to Red Tail 1, entering the craft smoothly.

Olivia hit the detonation key. The explosion sounded in all directions. Flames rose in the sky, and debris scattered everywhere. Ten seconds later, a shock wave hit the area sending water and soil flying.

"Is everyone ok?" Olivia asked. Before anyone could reply, the craft quaked and shook. Douglass moved toward the pilot seat, "Ma'am. We have been hit. Red Tail 1 is hit. I'll assess the damage."

Falling into the copilot seat, Zena checked the radar. "We're being followed by Aerofighter! That is who shot at us. And I think they are using micro plasma bombs. That's the only thing that would affect our craft! I'm putting Lady J on remote command. It will follow our lead. Mom, what should we do?"

Olivia looked at her daughter. "We have to get to safety and repair the craft. Can you take out the Aerofighter?"

"Douglass and I are doing that right now," Zena said.

"Well then, we need to get to the island. We can do the repairs and take care of any injuries there. Douglass is the island ready?" Olivia asked.

"Yes ma'am. It has been activated, and it is ready for us."

Marshall sat in one of the seats looking at his wife. He was weak from the continued electric shocks and tranquilizers he had received, but he had to say what he knew to be true. "He will follow us if he is alive. And since Aerofighter came for us, I am almost certain he is alive. He will try to kill me. He wants what I have."

Olivia looked at her husband, her brows knitted in a calculating line, and said, "Yes, husband, we will draw him out! We will bring him to our domain! And then we will take him down! That's the plan."

Mahalia looked at her grandmother, her face equally drawn and determined, "See you soon Grandfather Titus, see you soon." Malcolm looked at his family and nodded his head in agreement. He was determined to protect the family.

To be continued ...

Made in the USA
Middletown, DE
21 March 2022